Cassie's Castle

Jane Langford
Illustrated by Judy Spittle

SAO
Rigby

Contents

CHAPTER ONE

A Tall Story

It was Cassie's first day at her new school. She wanted a friend.

"Can I sit by you?" she asked a boy.

Alex nodded.

"I'm new here," said Cassie.

"Are you?" said Alex. "Where do you live?"

"I live in a castle," said Cassie.

Cassie didn't really live in a castle. She lived in a house.

"My castle has a tower," said Cassie. "A tall tower with a flag on top."

"Wow!" said Alex.

In fact, Cassie's house had a short chimney with a satellite dish on top.

"I keep dragons in the dungeons," said Cassie. "Big, fierce dragons."

Alex gasped.

Cassie didn't really keep dragons in the dungeons. She kept rabbits in a hutch—small, friendly rabbits.

"The dragons have green scales on their backs and long, spiky tails," said Cassie.

Cassie's rabbits had black spots on their backs and short, fluffy tails.

"It sounds wonderful," said Alex. "I'd like to see your castle. Can I come and visit you?"

"No," said Cassie.

"Why not?" asked Alex.

"The castle is only open to the public on holidays."

"Oh! Well, can I see one of your dragons?" asked Alex. "You could bring it to school tomorrow."

Cassie shook her head. "I can't bring a dragon to school," she said. "Dragons are dangerous."

"Oh, please!" said Alex.

"No," said Cassie. "Dragons have big teeth. They might bite the teacher."

Alex was disappointed. He had lots of storybooks about dragons. He knew that dragons could breathe fire and puff smoke.

"Dragons can fight knights in shining armor," said Alex.

"I know," said Cassie.

"They can kidnap beautiful princesses."

"I know," said Cassie.

"They can stand guard by caves full of treasure."

"I know," said Cassie. "But they can't come to school."

Alex sighed. He really wanted to see Cassie's dragons.

Chapter Two

My Lions

When it was time to go home, Alex asked Cassie, "Can I help you with your books?"

Cassie nodded. Alex wheeled Cassie's books nearly to her home.

"Stop!" said Cassie. "You can't come any further."

Alex frowned. "Why not?"

"Because of the lions," said Cassie.

"Lions!" said Alex. "What lions?"

"My lions," said Cassie. "They wait for me at the castle gate. They won't let anyone in except me."

There were no lions at Cassie's house. Her cat, Snowball, waited at the gate.

Snowball would let anyone in, as long as they tickled his tummy or scratched behind his ears.

Snowball was the sweetest cat in the whole world.

"I'm not scared of lions," said Alex.

"Well, you should be," said Cassie. "Lions have enormous teeth and terrible claws and very bad tempers."

"I don't care," said Alex. "I want to see where you live."

"No!" shouted Cassie.

Alex's eyes filled with tears. His lips wobbled.

"I'm sorry," said Cassie. "I didn't mean to shout. It's just that I don't want the lions to hurt you."

"They won't hurt me," said Alex. "Not if I give them a giant saucer of milk."

"Have you got any milk?" asked Cassie.

"No," said Alex.

"Then you'd better go home," said Cassie. "I'll see you tomorrow."

Cassie walked around the corner to her house.

Alex went home.

CHAPTER THREE

Sharks and Water Wings

At school the next day, Alex saw Cassie.

"Hello," he said. "How are the lions?"

"Hungry," said Cassie. "The lions are very hungry."

"Gee," said Alex. "That's too bad."

Cassie nodded, but she wasn't thinking of the lions.

She was thinking of her cat. Poor Snowball! Mom had forgotten to buy cat food.

"How are the dragons?" asked Alex.

"One escaped," said Cassie. "I had to chase him around the castle until I caught him again."

That wasn't quite true. Benjamin Rabbit had hopped out of his hutch. Cassie had chased him around the garden until he hopped back into his hutch.

"I'm glad you caught him," said Alex.

That afternoon, Alex waited for Cassie by the school gate. "Can I help you with your bag?" he asked.

"Of course," said Cassie.

Alex took Cassie's bag. It was very heavy.

"What have you got in here?" asked Alex.

"Lion food," said Cassie. "I bought it on the way to school."

Alex wanted to look, but Cassie wouldn't let him. It was actually cans of cat food for Snowball. Alex put the bag on his lap and wheeled it nearly all the way to Cassie's house.

"Stop!" said Cassie. "You can't come any further."

"Don't worry," said Alex. "I brought some milk today."

Cassie scowled. "That's no good."

"Why not?" asked Alex.

"You don't have anything for the sharks."

"Sharks! What sharks?" he asked.

Cassie looked surprised. "Haven't
I told you about the sharks?" she
said.

Alex shook his head.

Cassie told Alex that there was a moat in front of her castle. It was a very big moat, and full of water. Seven sharks swam in the water. "Big sharks," she said, "with enormous teeth."

Really, there was a fish pond in front of Cassie's house. It was just deep enough for Cassie's seven goldfish.

Cassie told Alex that sharks eat people.

Alex looked worried about the sharks.

So Cassie told him some more. She told him that the moat had a drawbridge. That was the only way to get into the castle. On Fridays, the man who lowered the drawbridge had the day off. Today was Friday.

"How will you get across the moat?" asked Alex.

"I'll have to swim," said Cassie.

"Swim?" Alex looked worried. "I'm not a very good swimmer," he said.

"I am," said Cassie. "I can swim really fast."

"Aren't you scared of the sharks?" asked Alex.

"No. Mom throws bread in for them. They like bread. I swim across when they're not looking."

"I could do that, too," said Alex.

"No, you couldn't," said Cassie. "You're not a very good swimmer, remember?"

Alex was embarrassed. "I can swim better with water wings," he said.

"What water wings?" asked Cassie. "I don't see any water wings. Have you got any with you?"

Alex shook his head.

"This is hopeless!" said Cassie. "Go home, Alex. I'll see you on Monday."

CHAPTER FOUR

Late for School

On Monday morning, Cassie was very late for school.

She grabbed her school bag and raced out onto the sidewalk, down the street, and around the corner. She bumped smack into Alex.

"Come on, Alex," said Cassie. "We're late for school."

"No we're not," said Alex. "We've got the day off."

"We do?" asked Cassie.

"Yes," said Alex. "It's a holiday, remember?"

Cassie looked worried.

"The castle is open today, isn't it?" he asked.

"Er, yes," said Cassie.

Alex pulled a bag off the back of his chair. He opened it.

"I've come prepared," he said.

Cassie looked in the bag.

"You've got milk for the lions?"

"Yes," said Alex.

"And bread for the sharks?"

"Yes," said Alex.

"And you've got water wings for swimming?"

"All blown up and ready," said Alex.

Cassie thought for a minute. Then she spoke.

"Follow me," she said.

Alex grinned. He followed Cassie down the street and around the corner.

Alex looked up the street. He looked down the street.

"I don't see a castle," he said.

"No," sighed Cassie.

"Should I look a little harder?" asked Alex.

Cassie pointed at her house.

"Is this the castle?" he asked.

"Er, yes," said Cassie.

"It's, um, a very nice castle," said Alex.

Cassie nodded solemnly.

"You'd better come in," she said.

Cassie and Alex went up the sidewalk to the gate.

CHAPTER FIVE

Benjamin Rabbit

"I'll have to be careful of the lions," said Alex.

"Um, yes," said Cassie.

Cassie opened the gate. Snowball was there. He pushed his head against Alex's leg and meowed.

"The lion!" said Alex. "Should I give him some milk?"

"All right," said Cassie.

Alex took the lid off the milk and poured some into Snowball's saucer.

Snowball purred.

Cassie walked down the garden path toward the pond. She looked embarrassed.

"This is the moat," she said.

Alex looked at the goldfish pond.

"I don't think I'll need my water wings today," he said.

"Not today," agreed Cassie.

"Of course not," said Alex, as he wheeled his way around the pond. "The drawbridge is down."

Cassie followed him. She stood on the other side and looked down.

"Should I feed the sharks?" asked Alex.

"Yes, please," answered Cassie.

Alex took some bread out of his bag. He tore it into little pieces, and tossed it into the water.

"Can I have some?" asked Cassie.

Alex tore off some bread and gave it to Cassie. They both threw the bread into the water. The goldfish loved it.

"Can I see the dragons now?" asked Alex.

Cassie looked hard at Alex. She wasn't very sure about showing him the dragons, but she knew just how much Alex wanted to see them.

Cassie took Alex around the house and out into the backyard. The rabbit hutch was in the middle of the lawn. Alex bent down over the hutch and looked in.

"These aren't the sort of dragons that fight knights in shining armor, are they?" asked Alex.

"No," said Cassie.

"Or the sort that kidnap beautiful princesses?"

"No."

"Or the sort that guard caves full of treasure?"

Cassie shook her head. She looked down at her toes. "No," she said. "They're not. Are you disappointed?"

"A little," said Alex. "Why did you tell so many lies?"

Cassie was ashamed. "I wanted a friend," she said.

Alex hugged Benjamin Rabbit tightly to his chest and smiled. "Did you want me to be your friend?" he asked.

"Yes," said Cassie.

"Well, why didn't you just ask?" said Alex.

"Just ask?"

"Of course," said Alex.

"Okay," said Cassie. "Will you be my friend?"

"Yes," said Alex. "But only if I can come and see your castle again on the next school holiday."

Cassie grinned. "You can come again tomorrow, if you like."